sheep

wool

trees

paper

AGATHA'S FEATHER BED

Not Just Another Wild Goose Story

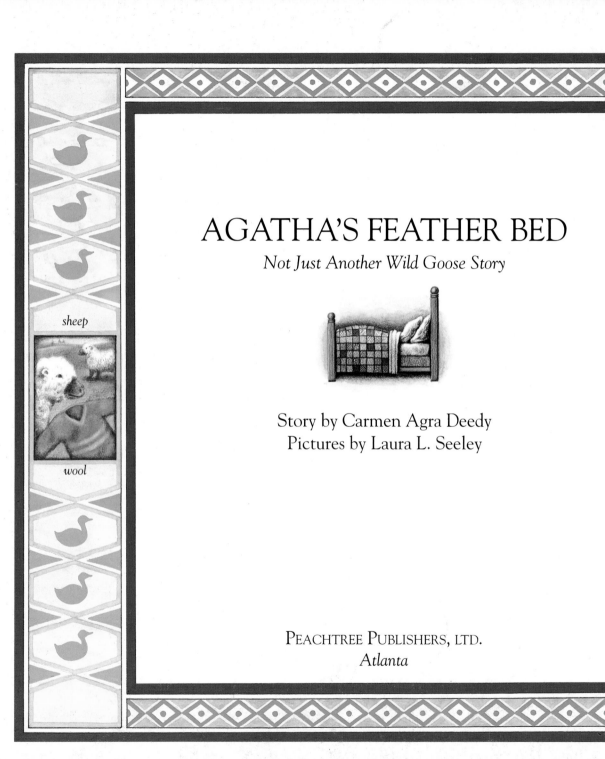

Story by Carmen Agra Deedy
Pictures by Laura L. Seeley

PEACHTREE PUBLISHERS, LTD.
Atlanta

To my husband and friend Shaun
and our dear daughters Katherine, Erin Grace, and Lauren

Published by
PEACHTREE PUBLISHERS, LTD.
494 Armour Circle, NE
Atlanta, Georgia 30324

Cover illustration by Laura L. Seeley
Design by Laura L. Seeley and Candace J. Magee

Manufactured in China

10 9 8 7 6 5

Library of Congress Cataloging in Publication Data

Deedy, Carmen Agra.
Agatha's feather bed : not just another wild goose story / story
by Carmen Agra Deedy ; pictures by Laura L. Seeley.
p. cm.
Summary: When Agatha buys a new feather bed and six angry naked geese show up to get
their feathers back, the incident reminds her to think about where things come from.
ISBN 1-56145-008-1 (hardcover)
ISBN 1-56145-096-0 (trade paper)
[1. Geese-fiction. 2. Conservation of natural resources-Fiction.] I. Seeley, Laura L., ill. II. Title.
PZ7.D3587Ag 1991
[E]--dc20   90-28257
                                                        CIP
                                                        AC

AGATHA'S FEATHER BED

Not Just Another Wild Goose Story

o you see that little shop sandwiched between two skyscrapers?

The shop belongs to my friend Agatha. She spins yarn and weaves cloth which she sells. The patterns she weaves are so amazing and the colors so beautiful that people come from all over Manhattan to buy her wares.

oysters

pearls

rubber tree

rubber

3

Agatha loves to talk, and she tells wonderful stories. In fact, you could say Agatha can spin a yarn better than anyone I know.

Here's one she told me the other day, and I know it must be true because even Agatha couldn't have made this one up:

One afternoon a little boy was shopping with his mother in Agatha's fabric shop. He was very bored and began playing with a shiny scrap of red cloth. Agatha leaned down and said to him, "That's silk. Do you know where it comes from?"

He shook his head.

cotton boll

cotton

dinosaurs

fossil fuel

5

silkworm cocoon

silk

cacao bean pods

chocolate

"It comes from worms," said Agatha.

"Worms!" he exclaimed.

"Why, yes. Silkworms," said Agatha.

"Wow . . . What kind of worm does this come from?" he asked, holding up a ball of purple cotton yarn.

"That's a very good question," Agatha replied. "That's cotton. And it doesn't come from a worm at all. It comes from a cotton boll that grows right out of the ground."

"What about the rest of this stuff?" asked the boy. "Does it come from neat places, too?"

"Oh, yes. This is wool, and it comes from—"

"—Sheep. That's easy."

"You're right," she said. "Now, this cloth is linen. Feel how stiff it is. I'll bet you can't guess where it comes from."

The boy thought and thought. Finally he asked, "Well, where *does* it come from?"

"A plant called flax," answered Agatha. "Let me tell you something I tell all my customers, especially children:

Everything comes from something,
Nothing comes from nothing.
Just like paper comes from trees,
And glass comes from sand,
An answer comes from a question.
All you have to do is ask."

It made the little boy smile.

That evening after everyone had gone home, Agatha went upstairs to her apartment. Several months earlier, she had ordered a new feather bed from her favorite catalog, B. B. Lean. It had just arrived that very day. Her old mattress was so lumpy and bumpy it was like sleeping on coal lumps and cherry pits.

Quickly she changed into her nightgown and brushed and flossed her teeth. She took out the tortoiseshell pins, and her long white hair fell,

and fell,

a n d   f e l l,

until it lay in little swirls around her feet.

tortoise

tortoiseshell

cow

dairy products

11

Then she brushed it with her boar-bristle brush. She never even finished her 100 strokes, she was so eager to try out her new mattress. She settled into bed, and in minutes she was asleep.

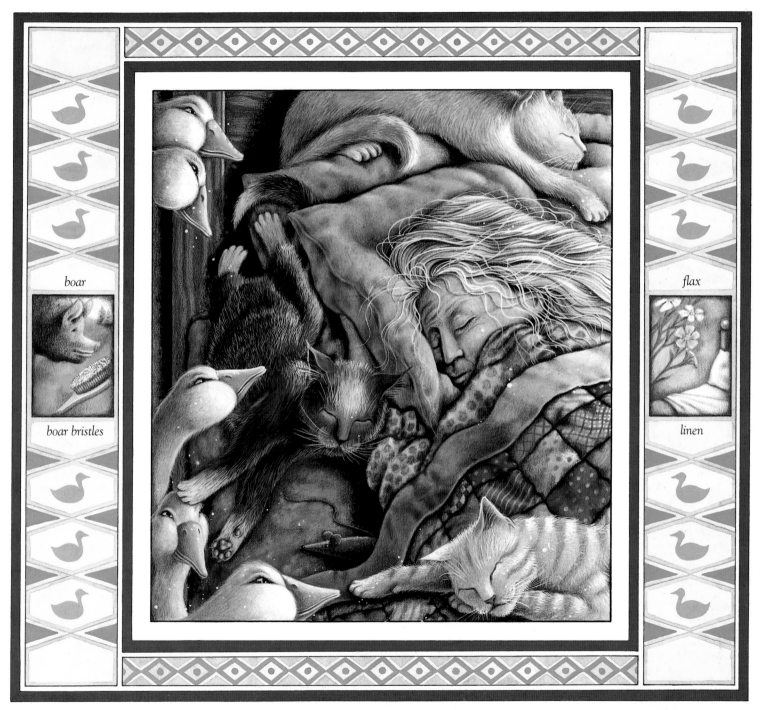

boar

boar bristles

flax

linen

Agatha dreamed that her room was filled with strange sounds: hushed whispers and the pitter patter of little feet. Suddenly she awoke with a start as she heard her window close with a thud.

She turned slowly in bed and saw that standing across her windowsill were . . .

sea

sea salt

flowers

perfume

15

six naked geese.

They were shivering in the cold and covered with goose bumps. She caught them just as they had ducked out.

Agatha stared and stared. You could have knocked her over with a feather.

At last, she opened the window and asked, "May I help you?"

The smallest goose, Sidney, stepped into the room. He pointed his pink little wing at Agatha's bed and said,

wheat

bread

sugar maple

syrup

reptiles

apparel

aloe plant

lotion

18

"We want our feathers back!"

"What?" asked Agatha.

"Feathers, Agatha, feathers. You know, we've been listening . . .

Everything comes from something,
Nothing comes from nothing.
Just like paper comes from trees,
And glass comes from sand.

The feathers in a feather bed don't grow on trees, my dear," he said.

"Where *did* you think the feathers in that feather bed came from?" asked the little goose.

Agatha looked at the bed and she looked at the geese and she looked at the bed and she looked at the geese.

Something in her sensed that her goose was cooked.

"I have to tell you we mean business, Agatha," said Sidney. "I wouldn't mess with a gaggle of angry, naked geese. We're not just a bunch of quacks. This could get ugly."

But Agatha had already made up her mind. She had worked hard to earn the money to buy that feather bed. And yet, she thought, what about those plucky little guys out there in the cold?

"I'll tell you what," said Agatha, a little down in the mouth. "Get back to me in three days. Trust me." And she gave them her credit card so they could book up at the Down Town Motel. Taking this as a sign of good will, they left quietly.

Naturally, she'd sent them on a wild goose chase.

Then she didn't waste a minute. She went downstairs to her sewing room, snatched her scissors, and got to work.

For three days, she didn't open her shop or speak to anyone.

sand

glass

coal

diamonds

And on the third night, just as they'd agreed, the geese came tapping at her window. This time Agatha was expecting them. She had left the window open, and she smiled to herself as they popped in, one by one.

"We're back, Agatha," said Sidney. "We had a great time with that credit card. They kept wanting to give us a bill, but we just said, 'No thanks, the last thing we need is another bill,' and then . . ."

But he never finished his sentence. As he looked across the room, he saw hanging on her wall were . . .

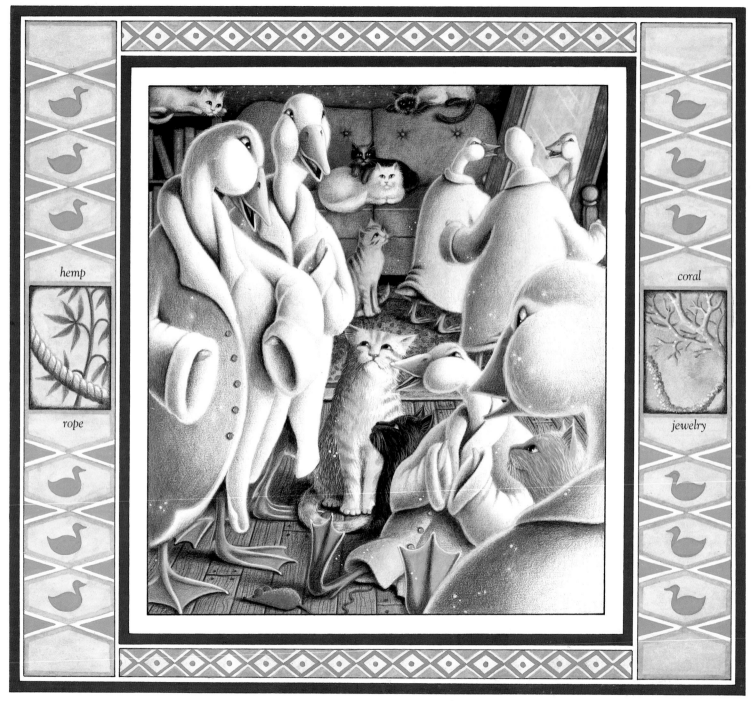

hemp

rope

coral

jewelry

six white, fleecy coats. Agatha had spun and woven and sewn each one.

The geese were extremely grateful and thanked her kindly. Each goose slipped into his new coat and took a gander in the mirror.

As they were about to leave, Sidney turned to Agatha and said, "You know, Agatha, these are really magnificent coats. Whatever did you make them from?"

Agatha sat up in her bed, and the geese saw that their coats were made from . . .

Agatha's hair.

And Agatha smiled and said,

"Everything comes from something. I have your feathers, you have my hair: What's good for the goose is good for the gander, eh, Sidney?"

"Oh, Agatha," said one of the geese. "You keep us in stitches."

"By the way, Agatha," added Sidney, chuckling, "your hair looks just ducky. And lucky for you and me, hair grows back . . . just like feathers."

bees and honeycomb

honey

elephant tusks

ivory

♦ ♦ ♦

Agatha says she's never heard another honk from her fine feathered friends. However, someone's been leaving fresh goose eggs on her doorstep every morning.

Where *do* goose eggs come from, anyway?

Author's Note

There are times when I feel so overwhelmed by the questions of my three young, articulate daughters that my only response is, "Go ask your father."

Yet, as parents and educators, we all know that asking questions and having them answered develops bright, inquisitive minds. AGATHA encourages children to ask about the origins of many commonplace things. This may send us scrambling headlong into the encyclopedia, where we might make some interesting discoveries.

Some answers may prove delightful; others, disturbing. What we choose to discuss with our children concerning ivory, whalebone, or the Brazilian rain forest is a matter of both individual conscience and collective responsibility.

But the first step is to ask.

© Paul Obregon

Carmen Deedy is a mesmerizing storyteller who has charmed children and adults alike throughout the United States and Canada. She contributes regular commentary to "Weekend All Things Considered." She is the author of THE LIBRARY DRAGON and TREEMAN, both from Peachtree Publishers.

• •

Laura L. Seeley, a native of Andover, Massachusetts, holds a degree in Fine Arts from the Rochester Institute of Technology.

© Sherrie Drury Jamison

She was twice named Georgia's Author of the Year for Juvenile Literature, in 1990 for her first book, THE BOOK OF SHADOWBOXES: *A Story of the ABC's*, and in 1992 for THE MAGICAL MOONBALLS, both from Peachtree Publishers. THE BOOK OF SHADOWBOXES was also recently released as a multimedia book on CD-ROM by IBM/EduQuest.

Seeley illustrated CHRISTMAS AND THE OLD HOUSE by Tom T. Hall and wrote and illustrated McSPOT'S HIDDEN SPOTS, *A Puppyhood Secret,* which are also from Peachtree.

• •

Special Thanks To:

Tersi Bendiburg
Mami y Papi
Maggie Winfrey
Ruth Ann Hendrickson
Clark Orwick
Susan Thurman
Laurie Seeley
and the women of the Peachtree Spinners Guild,
who took me under their wing.